ALMOST UNCIRCULATED

by

LEVON VEGA

ALMOST UNCIRCULATED
Copyright © 2018, Levon Vega

All Rights Reserved

ISBN: 978-0-578-20716-2

Any references to historical events, real people, or real places are used fictitiously. Names, characters, and places are products of the author's imagination.

Levon Vega
Seattle, WA 98108
Email: Vegartruth@gmail.com

Revised Edition, 2018

www.levonvega.com

CHARACTERS
(By ACT/ORDER OF APPEARANCE)

ACT I

BEN	50s, white, coin dealer, inventory is quantity over quality.
GRACE	50s, white, wife of Ben, neurotic.
WAITER	34, seemingly overqualified.
OLDER MAN	50, Ukrainian, quiet.
NAZAR	50, Ukrainian coin thief, sees himself as the handsome brother.
LUIS	29, Puerto Rican, Retail coin business owner.
EMPLOYEE	20s, female, front desk employee.
JOEY	40s, shady character.
TEDDY	40s, white, coin collector who is seen at most conventions, sweet guy, longtime friend of Luis.

MR. FISCHER	65, Greek collector, hard ass, nothing anyone else sells is good enough for his collection.
DONALD	60s, white, intelligent, socially awkward.
HERMAN BENSIN	70, African-American, soft spoken and driven.
BARTENDER	20s, African-American woman with a kind smile.
SCRAP	20s, hustler, friend of Herman.
MRS. BENSIN	67, African-American, assertive and generous.
RHONA	26. Swedish-American., columnist for the local paper.

ACT II

VADIM	46, Ukrainian, coin thief, fit and has "the looks."
JERRY	34, blue jean wearing American, skilled thief.
IGGY	30. Ukrainian-American, nephew of Vadim, son of Nazar, he is "the helper."

FINN	Late 20s, Irish-American loan shark, high-school best friend of Luis.
CESAR	55, Argentinian Nightclub owner, slicked hair and V-neck shirt, husband of Rhona's mother.
GAYLE	50, Swedish immigrant, Rhona's mother.
TINA	20s, waitress, sweet and helpful but gullible.

ACT III

OFFICER DOYLE	Late 40s, experienced officer who has done his time and knows everyone in town. Captain once called him the sweetest guy to ever wear a badge.
OFFICER ZAREMBA	Late 20s, clean cut young cop, knows the rules and would rather follow them.

SCENES

ACT I
"I REBUILT THIS THING FROM THE GROUND UP"

Scene 1	Rest Stop/Dining Area
Scene 2	Convention
Scene 3	Bo Peep's/Bensin's House
Scene 4	Luis's Coin Shop

ACT II
"BROTHERS, FRIENDS, AND THE AMERICAN…"

Scene 1   Safehouse

Scene 2   Luis's Coin Shop

Scene 3   Lulu's Bar

Scene 4   Secluded Parking Lot

Scene 5   Café/Coin Shop

ACT III
"ALMOST UNCIRCULATED"

Scene 1   Rhona's Office

Scene 2   Convenience Store/Back Lot

Scene 3   Bensin House

Scene 4   Bensin House Hallway

Scene 5   Stage

ALMOST UNCIRCULATED

Setting: Luis stands on a small stage in a downtown bookstore. For his afternoon book reading, the room has been arranged with rows of chairs facing toward him. He steps up to an easel supporting a whiteboard and writes a list of words with the heading: COIN GRADES.

LUIS

Alright, we ready? (Pause) I'd say it all boils down to the fact that I rebuilt this thing from the ground up. Before he died, my uncle worked day in, day out, for years so we didn't have to. (Pause) I don't know. I'm alright now. I guess I'm strong after all of it, but it took a while. Some of the most important moments of my life felt like they took hours to pass like a tornado in slow motion. I never knew I had the ability to write this story but, I treated it like it was the most important deal of my life and somehow it worked out.

> (Luis points to the board with his marker then circles a word.)

Uncirculated. It means exactly what you would think. However, Almost Uncirculated (points) that's a little different. Just short of beautiful, one step away from awesome, almost as lustrous as when it left the mint. Interesting—the reality of coming up short. It's funny how things can be impressive, but not quite. This afternoon we are going on a trip. That way you all can see the heartbreak I went through before I could finally say that I made it. There are smudges and scratches on this story, but I hope you all enjoy it anyway.

(Luis sits at the table with his book.)

Thanks. Thank you all for coming.

("I REBUILT THIS THING FROM THE GROUND UP")

ACT 1, SCENE 1

Setting: Late at night, Ben and Grace, an older couple, are the only ones seated in a small dining area at a rest stop gas station.

WAITER

Here's your coffee and I'll be right back with that pie.

(Waiter walks away.)

BEN

Thank you.

GRACE

Well, Darlin', it looks like we're already half-way home.

BEN

Yeah, we are. And better yet, we made some money.

GRACE

Did we sell all those silver coins?

BEN

Everything but the expensive pair.

GRACE

Maybe business is getting better after all.

BEN

I hope so. I don't want to close our store.

> (The couple look out the
> window while sipping their
> coffee.)

BEN

Do you see someone over by our car?

> (Grace shifts her body as
> she looks.)

GRACE

I don't see anyone.

BEN

Look! Right there!

> (Ben stands and begins
> walking toward the front
> door.)

> (A man is now seen outside
> the front door. He locks the
> door with a chain before
> Ben pushes it.)

BEN

Let me out of here!

GRACE

What was that, Ben? What's happening?

BEN

(Ben looks around.)

Waiter! Waiter! Someone is robbing us!

GRACE

Honey, what do we do?

BEN

I don't know, Grace. Go back there and find someone!

GRACE

Oh, I'm scared!

BEN

Honey, they got all our inventory out there. Do something!

(Grace scrambles to find someone and knocks a table over.)

BEN

(Ben screams at the unseen robbers through the glass storefront.)

Motherfuckers, you're gonna pay for this! Put that down!

(A loud bang is heard from
the kitchen which drives
Grace away. She grabs Ben
in fear and cries.)

GRACE

Ben, do something!

BEN

I'm trying!

(Another loud crash causes
the couple to stop and turn
around.)

GRACE

Hello? Someone is robbing us... Please... Please
help!

(An older man slowly
walks out from the kitchen
with a rope in his hand.)

BEN
(Ben turns to look at the
robbers and then back at
the man.)

GRACE

Ben! Who is that? Honey?

(The older man laughs at
the couple.)

BEN
(Ben speaks slowly while
keeping his eyes on the
man.)

I don't know, Grace. But, just do what he asks.

ACT I, SCENE 2

Setting: A lavish downtown hotel bustling with people. The late autumn decor doesn't quite mix with the futuristic interior. A family sits on a couch waiting for a shuttle to arrive. Luis, well-dressed, walks through the door like he owns the place. He approaches an employee at the front desk.

LUIS
Hey there.

EMPLOYEE
How may I help you, sir?

LUIS
I'm here for the coin show.

EMPLOYEE
Oh, of course. It's right down that hallway.

LUIS
Thank you.

(Luis walks confidently
through the long corridor.
He smirks, and a few other
businessmen nod their
heads and make comments.
He approaches Joey.)

JOEY

Hey, Luis, you got that?

LUIS
(Luis steps closer to Joey.)

Yeah Joe, here you go.

(Luis pulls an envelope
from his blazer and hands
it to him.)

(The bourse floor is a busy
trading pit laid out across
the hotel's finest ballroom.
Hundreds of tables are set
up with men selling coins
and paper money to
collectors and
businessmen.)

LUIS
(Luis enters the bourse
floor and walks toward his
table.)

Hey there, Teddy.

TEDDY

Oh man, there he is. I had no idea you were coming.

LUIS

Oh yeah.

TEDDY

How are you with Ben and all that?

LUIS

What do you mean?

TEDDY

Ben and Grace from Pennsylvania. You guys aren't close?

LUIS

I don't know 'em.

TEDDY

Ah, well, they were robbed yesterday coming back from the White Plains show.

LUIS

Was it a lot?

TEDDY

Everything.

LUIS

That's rough man. Send my best, if you know
them like that. How's Troy doing?

TEDDY
(Teddy grins and tilts his
head.)

He's great. A little sick right now, but his mother
is taking care of him.

LUIS

That's great.

TEDDY

Yeah. (beat) You have anything for me this trip?

LUIS

I don't think so, but I'll take a look. I have my
hands in a collection back home.

TEDDY

Please, Luis. You always find the good stuff.

LUIS

Yeah.

(Luis laughs.)

I'll give you a call.

TEDDY

Great, I'll stop by a little later.

LUIS

Perfect. I'm table 7-0-7.

>
> (Luis walks away. Luis
> continues to gauge his
> surroundings and after a
> moment arrives at his
> table.)

>
> CUSTOMER
> (A customer speaks to Luis
> in a gravelly voice.)

Hey guy.

LUIS

Mr. Fischer.

>
> (Luis removes his hat and
> places it and his things on
> the back table. Luis pulls
> out a pocket folder from
> his bag.)

MR. FISCHER

Jeez, kid. I was about to go over to Louisville
Rare Coins.

LUIS

Yeah? He ain't got nothing over there.

>
> (Luis sits down across
> from Mr. Fischer.)

MR. FISCHER
Hey, you're probably right.

LUIS
How have you been? Retiring anytime soon?

MR. FISCHER
Shit, I'd probably quicker drop dead. Have you
seen Tanya, my shop girl?

LUIS
(Luis chuckles.)

Not yet, man.

MR. FISCHER
Oh man, you should swing by the store
sometime.

LUIS

Yeah?

MR. FISCHER
Yeah. She's one of those mixed girls. Make you
lose your shoes.

LUIS
(Luis laughs his ass off.)

You're too much. I hope I'm as driven as you at
your age.

MR. FISCHER
I know it. Whatcha got for me?

LUIS
(Luis opens the folder and
pulls out a bundle of paper
money and ten or so coins.
Luis then fans out the bills
and spreads the coins
across the empty
showcase.)

There.

MR. FISCHER
(Mr. Fischer looks at the
bills and coins and then
removes his glasses.
Chewing the bow, he looks
at Luis with narrow eyes.)

Where is it?

LUIS
Where's what?

MR. FISCHER
The coins you called me about. You know I don't
collect any of this stuff.

(Luis smiles and slips his
two fingers into his shirt
pocket. He pulls out the

coin and holds it in front of
his chest.)

MR. FISCHER
Don't bait me boy. I have Tanya for that.

(Luis laughs and hands the
coin to Fischer. Mr.
Fischer uses his loupe to
inspect the coin before
speaking.)

MR. FISCHER
Was it cleaned?

LUIS
Nope. Doesn't look it.

MR. FISCHER
And it's not stolen, is it?

LUIS
You know what? I forgot that I have a customer
back home for that one.

MR. FISCHER
Don't play me like that, Luis.

LUIS
I don't want to. You're good to me.

MR. FISCHER
I know I am.

LUIS

You like it or not?

MR. FISCHER
(Mr. Fischer sighs.)

She's better than I thought. When you called, I
wasn't sure, but (beat) not bad.

LUIS

Well, the last bad coin I owned was a Christmas
present.

MR. FISCHER
(Mr. Fischer grins and
continues studying his
crush.)

I like it kid.

LUIS

I know.

MR. FISCHER

Give me the number.

LUIS

Hold on a second. Let me see what I paid.

(Luis steps over to his back
table to find his price list.

Luis figures the price and
turns back around.)

MR. FISCHER
Alright! Don't kill me, you hear?

LUIS
(Luis returns to Mr.
Fischer.)

My best price to a guy like you is $27,000.

MR. FISCHER
Hell, you must not like me then.

LUIS
Now you know that thing's worth thirty easy.

MR. FISCHER
I know, I know.

LUIS
But I'd rather sell it to you than the auction.

(Mr. Fischer sits back and
waits before saying
anything. Luis waits then
picks up the coin.)

LUIS
Hey, Donald! Come here a sec.

(Luis waves to a man in the
aisle behind Mr. Fischer.
The man is wearing thick
glasses and is older than
Luis and Mr. Fischer. He
also looks like he has
library-sized knowledge on
coins.)

DONALD
(Stuttering.)

Y-y-yes?

LUIS

What's this coin worth?

DONALD
(Stuttering.)

Well, umm, y-y-you know it has been a while
now, b-b-but gauging the metals and…

LUIS

Ballpark.

DONALD
(Donald looks over at
Luis's name tag. Stuttering
a bit.)

Well…L-l-luis, do you need a r-r-retail value?

LUIS

Yeah, sure.

DONALD
(Stuttering.)

Hmm, let's see. I c-c-could go ahead and p-p-pay twenty-eight thousand.

(Mr. Fischer looks over at
Luis confused.)

LUIS

Shit, you got that kind of cash laying around?

(Mr. Fischer becomes
worried and begins
shuffling through his
things.)

DONALD
(Stuttering.)

Umm, y-y-yeah. My check is g-g-good. You can ask…

LUIS

Sorry, Don. It's a gift for someone.

DONALD

Alright.

LUIS

Stay there, Mr. Fischer.

(Luis walks back behind
his table and faces Mr.
Fischer.)

LUIS

There you go, boss. She's yours.

MR. FISCHER

You scared me for a second there.

LUIS
(Luis chuckles.)

No! I did? I just wanted a second opinion.

MR. FISCHER
(Mr. Fischer pulls out a
checkbook, fills out a
check, and slides it to Luis
who is standing across
from him. Mr. Fischer
picks up the coin.)

Thanks, guy. I might be around again before
Sunday.

LUIS
(Luis folds the check and
slides it into his shirt
pocket.)

Good luck out there.

(Mr. Fischer walks away
into the cross section
carrying his cane, but not
using it. He nods in
approval and looks
around.)

ACT I, SCENE 3

Setting: 1966. In a jazz club called Bo Peep's that plays
hard bop jazz music. It is night time and the bar is tightly
packed. A man in a suit leans over the bar to talk to the
female bartender.

HERMAN BENSIN

Good evening, baby.

BARTENDER

Hey there, Hun. What do ya need?

HERMAN BENSIN

Hmm, be a doll and bring us two gins in about
five.

BARTENDER

Of course.

(Herman walks through the
dance floor. He nods his
head to the bass player of
the band that is tight on a
small stage. He enters a

small, dimly lit back room.
There are fewer people
there. Herman steps up to a
small group of his friends
who are all laughing.)

SCRAP

No, but you don't understand. It's different. When
a child's in the mix you gotta act as if you really
do care. I mean, I care, but I just can't stand the
mother.

HERMAN BENSIN
(Herman grabs the
woman's elbow and looks
at Scrap.)

What now, Scrap? You get in on the wrong side
of a deal and now these lovely people have to
hear your silliness?

SCRAP

Perfect, Herman. You know how it is! She's
doing this for a reason. She's wanting me to
move out.

HERMAN BENSIN

I know, buddy, calm down.

(Herman kisses the woman
on the cheek and puts his
arm around her waist,
leading her away.)

MRS. BENSIN

Bye, guys.

SCRAP

Man, that's cold.

> (Herman and the woman
> walk away to a quiet table
> illuminated by a hanging
> light above.)

> MRS. BENSIN
> (Mrs. Bensin turns around
> in search of the waitress
> and notices she is already
> approaching with their
> drinks. Mrs. Bensin looks
> back at Herman, who is
> flipping a coin.)

Again, with the coin?

> HERMAN BENSIN
> (Herman laughs gently.
> The waitress places the
> sweaty glasses on the table.
> She then takes the dollar
> and walks away.)

Thank ya'.

> (To Mrs. Bensin.)

Now, what's the matter, Darling?

MRS. BENSIN

It's just that, you look like a money man of some
kind.

HERMAN BENSIN

You know I'm no trouble. I just like my coins.

(Mrs. Bensin rolls her
eyes.)

The way I see it. It's my little slice of privilege.
And I know that means something to you, too.

MRS. BENSIN

I guess it's cute. I just don't want anyone getting
the wrong idea.

HERMAN BENSIN
(Herman rubs Mrs.
Bensin's arm with his
hand.)

They won't, Honey. How was class?

MRS. BENSIN

Not bad. The professor is looking to start a club.
I might join.

HERMAN BENSIN

That's grand.

MRS. BENSIN

How was work?

HERMAN BENSIN

Well, I'm thinking of leaving pretty soon.

MRS. BENSIN

Wait, why?

HERMAN BENSIN

A friend of mine is making alright money selling the coins. I was hoping to start up a business for myself.

MRS. BENSIN

I hope you're joking.

> (Herman takes a big sip of his gin.)

I ain't gonna spend my life with no boy scout. I need a man.

> (Herman removes a cigarette from his shirt pocket. Herman tilts his head, lights the cigarette with his table candle, and blows a bit of smoke her way, but stays silent. Herman exits. Mrs. Bensin follows.)

(Mrs. Bensin walks behind
the wall. Lighting fades to
dark.)

Setting: Modern day. Lighting comes on to show Mrs.
Bensin's living room, cleanly decorated with real wood
furniture from the 1970s and family pictures. Mrs. Bensin
and Luis enter from behind the wall.

MRS. BENSIN
(Laughing)

You got the wrong idea, baby. Only people in the
family are me and Herman, and Herman's gone.

LUIS
Alright, Mrs. Bensin. Just making sure. I don't
want to buy anything I'm not meant to.

MRS. BENSIN
Well, you're not.

LUIS

Perfect.

MRS. BENSIN
It's been willed to me. Here's the list with the
names and numbers of the silly things.

LUIS

Thank you.

(Luis pulls the box of coins
toward him and opens the
folder.)

MRS. BENSIN
Now more importantly, would you care for a
drink?

LUIS
Sure. Whatever you have, Mrs. Bensin.

MRS. BENSIN
Well, sweet tea is what I have.

LUIS
My favorite.

(Grinning, Luis flips
through the handwritten
pages of Herman's list of
every coin and description
to match his collection. He
then comes to a letter that
reads as follows.)

HERMAN BENSIN
(Voice-over reading the
letter: I am probably dead
by now, but I hope you
enjoy my collection. I
worked hard for years with
this treasure hunt and gave
a lot of money to a lot of
men like you to no avail.

So, if you are buying this
collection, I ask that you
only pay my wife less than
half of what it's worth. You
know this business and are
doing what I never could.
She never took me
seriously anyway. Enjoy.)

(Luis nervously fumbles
the papers.)

MRS. BENSIN
(Off stage.)

I hope there's something good in that silly box.
God knows it's probably a hundred dollars.

(Mrs. Bensin laughs
ridiculously to herself.)

LUIS
Yeah, give me a few and I'll tally it up.

(Luis pulls the box toward
him and scans the rest. He
then puts the papers into
his briefcase and chugs
down his iced tea. He looks
over at a framed photo who
can only be Herman for a
moment.)

LUIS
(Calling out)

Alright!

MRS. BENSIN
(She walks over from
doing the dishes.)

Was anything there?

LUIS
Yeah, it looks like I can pay twenty-five
thousand for the box.

MRS. BENSIN
Oh gosh, maybe Herman did know something.
(Beat)Doubt it, though. He was probably just
guessing, right? I mean, who'd spend a hundred
dollars on a coin that says it's worth a dollar?

LUIS
Yeah

(Fake smile.)

Probably.

(He then writes his check,
hands it to Mrs. Bensin,
and picks up his boxes.)

MRS. BENSIN

Come on, Luis. I'll get the door.

LUIS

Thank you so much, Mrs. Bensin. And thanks for
the tea.

MRS. BENSIN
(She holds the door for
Luis.)

Any time, honey. Tell Rhona I said hello.

LUIS

Sure will.

(Luis descends the steps
and walks down the road.)

ACT I, SCENE 4

Setting: Luis's shop. A few people walk outside where
Christmas decorations flood Main Street. The coin store is
empty and the lights dim. Sign reads CLOSED.

LUIS
(Luis enters with his new
purchases. He lays them on
the showcase.)

Honey?

(Silence)

LUIS

Rhona!

(Some sounds are heard
from the bathroom in the
back of the store.)

LUIS
(Luis nudges the bathroom
door lightly.)

Hun?

RHONA

Yeah?

LUIS
(Luis pushes the door the
rest of the way.)

Who are you all dressed up for?

RHONA

Eh, just trying it on. How do ya like it?

LUIS

It's nice.

RHONA

Ann made it for me.

                    LUIS
Hmm. Ann…

                    RHONA
From the green, she has the horse statue out
front.

                         (Luis puts his arm around
                         her.)

                    LUIS
That's right.

                         (Luis sits on the toilet.
                         Rhona looks back into the
                         mirror and fixes her hair.)

It's too sexy to wear outside, though.

                         (Rhona shoots him a
                         "c'mon now" look and then
                         shakes her head. Luis
                         cranes his head down and
                         glances up trying to see up
                         Rhona's dress.)

                    RHONA
How'd it go with Mrs. Bensin?
                    LUIS
You know, she had some pretty good stuff.

                         (Luis stands and steps past
                         her.)

(Luis walks out to his
showcase and looks
through a box of
inventory.)

RHONA

Oh, yeah? I thought it'd be all those…uh…state
quarters.

LUIS

No, her husband had a pretty good collection.

(Silence from Rhona)

LUIS

It was strange though. I found a letter with his
stuff and it was like he was trying to talk to me.

RHONA

Hmm weird. He was a quiet guy from what I
remember. I never saw them together though.

LUIS

Yeah. You're right.

RHONA
(Rhona exits the bathroom.
She pulls a framed article
from the wall.)

What's this, mister?

LUIS

Oh, yeah. I finally found one that fits.

RHONA

That was so long ago. I can't believe I wrote it that way.

LUIS

"Young business man breaks downtown mold."

RHONA

Gimme!

LUIS

"After the death of Tino Montanez, the only coin store in town has been revamped, but remains in the family."

RHONA

Baby! Put it down. Please.

(Rhona grasps for the article.)

LUIS

Nope. It's going back on the wall.

(Luis hangs it back up.)

LUIS

I like it. Look at it every day.

RHONA

OK, Honey. Let me know how the meeting goes.
I gotta head out.

LUIS

Yeah, Babe. Of course.

RHONA

I'll be at home when you're done.

LUIS

Yep. Be careful out there.

> (Rhona smiles and kisses
> him then exits the shop.
> Lights go dark.)

Setting: The stage is dark except for spotlight on Luis on
the left and a spotlight on a coin dealer on the right. Luis is
talking to the coin dealer on the phone.

LUIS

Hey, there, it's Luis. You in town?

DEALER

What do you have?

LUIS

I have it all. I'm at the store.

> (Luis pours a cup of coffee
> from a pot near his desk.)

DEALER

I'm close. I'll see you soon, Luis.

LUIS

Alright. It's two doors down from the diner.

("BROTHERS, FRIENDS,
AND THE
AMERICAN...")

ACT II, SCENE 1

Setting: The safe house where the thieves gather is well kept. Aside from the coins and paper money stacked on various surfaces, there isn't much in the way of decorations. A simplified, yet colorful painting from the 1980s hangs above the couch.

            VADIM
            (Vadim walks through the
            safe house and sits next to
            Jerry who is busy counting
            money. He pulls a
            photograph from his wallet
            and places it in front of
            Jerry with a smile.)

First man I killed.

            JERRY
What are you crazy?

            (Vadim laughs.)

            VADIM
Listen kid, I grew up poor and this man was the one holding our family down.

JERRY

Who was it?

VADIM

My father's boss. He would make a strong
welder come home and cry. Father worked until
he was fucking delirious and forgot who his
children were.

JERRY

I'm sorry, V.

VADIM

Nope, don't be sorry. We helped him retire early.

JERRY
(Jerry laughs)

Alright.

VADIM

What I'm saying is if you're going to do this you
need to remember the first man who kicked you
while you were down, or you'll never win.

(Iggy enters in sporty
clothing. He looks at Jerry
from behind his back.)

IGGY

Hey Uncle, I came to watch over the uh...oh
sorry...

(Vadim rolls his eyes and
shake his head. Iggy grabs
a Danish from the counter.)

IGGY

Ah, I love it.

JERRY

Love what?

IGGY

When you count our money.

JERRY
(Jerry looks up.)

So do I, but this is my money.

VADIM

Hey, I don't want to hear that shit.

(Vadim stands.)

Work it out!

(Vadim stares long at Iggy
and then walks toward the
door.)

(Jerry rubber bands his
cash and marks it with a
pencil.)

JERRY

You out of here, boss?

VADIM

Yeah. I'm already late. I'm meeting with
someone.

JERRY

Have fun. Hey, here's your picture.

VADIM

Keep it. We share enemies here.

(Vadim exits the room.)

IGGY

If you are stealing, Father will kill you too quick.

JERRY

We did the diner job together. Don't these guys
tell you anything?

IGGY

I know. (Pause) OK? I know about the diner job.

JERRY

So, if you did that job, you'd have this money.

IGGY

I don't need that little job. We have something
big coming. You will beg to be a part of this.

JERRY

(Jerry laughs.)

Have fun.

IGGY

You are a rat. I don't see why my uncle hired you
anyway.

JERRY
(Jerry stands.)

It's because I know how to do this shit in my
sleep.

(Iggy steps up to Jerry and
pushes him. Jerry loses his
balance, but quickly
regains it.)

JERRY

Oooh, wrong move buddy boy.

IGGY

Fucking American.

(Jerry pushes Iggy against
the wall with his forearm
on his throat. Jerry laughs
through his teeth.)

OK. Get off me!

JERRY

Don't play with me, alright?

IGGY

Damn it! You're an asshole.

(Iggy catches his breath.)

JERRY

Oh, I'm sure of it.

IGGY

You better watch out now.

JERRY

Yeah, calm down. I ain't gonna hurt ya.

(Iggy shakes his head and
pulls out his phone. He
walks toward the kitchen
and Jerry walks out the
front door.)

ACT II, SCENE 2

Setting: Luis's shop, lit by only one light. The rest of the
light shines in from the streetlights and gleaming electric
Christmas lights wrapped tightly around the rows of trees
along the street. Luis works at his showcase getting various
items ready for resale. Vadim knocks on the front window.
His hand is flat above his eyes as he searches for Luis
within the store.

VADIM

Open up, buddy.

                    LUIS
I'm coming.

                    (Luis opens the door.)

                    VADIM
You have very nice store, man.

                    LUIS
Thanks. I'm the only one in town, I gotta be
good.

                              (The two men shake
                              hands.)

                    VADIM
Right, only one.

                              (Vadim snoops around.)

                    VADIM
So, what do you have? You told me gold and
silver, yes?

                    LUIS
                    (Luis steps behind the
                    showcase and looks in the
                    man's eyes.)

Yeah, I have some good stuff. It's a good deal,
too, for wholesale.

                              (Vadim moves some things
                              around in the open

briefcase. Luis spins it
toward him and looks
inside.)

LUIS

And if you got the money, it's all yours.

(Vadim laughs
cartoonishly. Luis begins
extracting boxes of gold
coins.)

LUIS

This stuff's right out of the weeds. Take a look.

VADIM

You know the price is based always on the grade.

LUIS

(Luis takes a deep breath.)

Of course. You think I'm an idiot?

VADIM

Look friend, don't worry. This is business.

(Vadim walks to another
case and begins looking at
something completely
unrelated.)

LUIS

Listen. I know what business is and I know what
my inventory is worth.

VADIM

Yeah, alright. (Beat) You are still young.

LUIS

Oh, man.

VADIM

What?

LUIS

Are you hoping to buy anything or just stick your oily hands in my shit and try to act like your knowledge exceeds my own?

>   (Vadim reaches into the
>   back of his jeans begins
>   pulling out a pistol. Luis
>   hears a loud knock at the
>   back door.)

LUIS

Excuse me. I'll be right back.

>   (Luis steps away and opens
>   the back door.)

LUIS

Finn?

Setting: Back alley behind the coin shop. It is dark and quiet. A few lights illuminate the two men standing parallel to the brick wall.

FINN
(Finn does not answer but
pulls Luis toward him.)

Be quiet.

LUIS

What are you...

FINN

Shut up.

LUIS
What the fuck are you doing? Is this a joke?

FINN
(Finn looks around.)

Quiet! You'll thank me for this.

(Finn guides Luis around
the corner and forces him
into a blacked-out car. He
then scans the area before
entering.)

LUIS
C'mon man. What's going on?

(Finn takes out a cigarette
and then lights it.)

LUIS

Can you fucking hear me?

FINN

What's going on? Of course, you don't know
what's going on! What were you doing in there?

LUIS

I was doing a deal.

FINN

With who?

LUIS

Some asshole. And now because of you, he's
probably robbing me!

FINN

Because of me, you're alive! (Beat) That bastard
had a loaded snub in his pocket.

LUIS
(Luis ponders this. The
men stop yelling.)

What do you mean?

FINN

Do you even know his name?

LUIS

No. I just had his business card. He told me once
that he buys wholesale.

FINN

Well, he's one of the Liski brothers. Biggest coin thieves of the East coast. (Beat) They find guys like you selling collections and bury them.

LUIS

Shit.

FINN

Yeah, you remember Ben Montgomery at all? He had a store up in P-A.

LUIS

Sounds familiar. Didn't he get shot leaving a...

FINN

Exactly. Then they tied his wife up and choked her to death.

LUIS

How do you know so much?

FINN

Well, I was in town and I saw you doing a late-night deal. Then I saw Nazar and knew he had a heavy pocket. He wasn't planning on paying.

LUIS

And these Liski brothers? Who are these guys?

FINN

Nazar, the older one, did twenty years for killing
his cousin. He's a kid in a killer's body.

LUIS

Have you done business with 'em?

FINN

If you can call it that. The guys fucked me over a
few months back on a loan. So, I sold their only
safehouse.

>   (Luis pauses. He keeps
>   thinking. The car stops.)

FINN

Look, I just saw a friend in need and did
something about it.

LUIS

Son-of-a-bitch. So, I ain't gonna see that
collection again?

FINN

I'll see what I can do. Where are you gonna go?

LUIS

I'll go to Lulu's down the street.

FINN

What's that? A strip club?

LUIS

No, it's my father-in-law's place over on State
Street.

FINN

Right. I heard it's a shithouse at night. Cops over
there twice a week.

LUIS

You know how my people are, Man.

FINN

Oh, yeah, I forgot your mom married a Rican
before settling with Sullivan.

                              (Luis opens his door. Both
                              men exit.)

FINN

Listen, Brother. We're gonna find these guys.

LUIS
                    (Luis shakes his head.)
You think so?

FINN

We'll work on it. (Beat) You got a gun?

LUIS

Yeah.

FINN

You sure?

                    LUIS
Yeah, it's behind the… Wait, no, it's next to the
safe.

                    FINN
Alright. So, any of these scumbags come around,
at least you're good.

                    LUIS
I can't believe this shit.

                    FINN
I know. Now if anything happens… (Beat) You
listening?

                    (Finn nudges Luis.)

                    LUIS
Yeah.

                    FINN
You call me before anyone else. No cops. You
call me.

                    (The two men shake
                    hands.)

                    LUIS
Thanks, Finn.

ACT II, SCENE 3

Setting: Lulu's Bar is small and decorated in a modest Latino fashion. The late-night crowd is well watered and chatting. A man is playing Spanish piano music. Luis enters through the back door shaking his head. He passes the man playing piano. Lights drop. Spotlight on Luis. The rest of the characters sit still in very low light.

LUIS
(Luis looks around.)

Damn it! Alright, so as you can see, it's not going so well right now.

(Luis takes a shot from the bar.)

I've lost about (tallies) fifty thousand fucking dollars and my best friend is the only reason I'm still alive. (Beat) Screw that, I don't need him though. Thanks a lot, Finn. Asshole. (Long pause) Anyway, these two people are probably worth introducing. Gayle is the mother of my beautiful bride. She escaped a violent marriage in Sweden and brought Rhona here for a new life. She's always been critical of my job, but now it looks like she was right. And this guy, Cesar, that's my guy. I tell ya, a good father-in-law is worth a lot. He'll get you out of worlds of trouble, believe me.

Anyway, now that you guys have met, let's get back to it.

(Luis throws a dollar in the
piano player's tip jar and
the whole place wakes
back up. Music back, lights
up.)

                    LUIS
Shit, shit, shit!

                    GAYLE
Honey.

                    LUIS
Hey, Ma! How's everything?

                    CESAR
Luis! ¿Como estas?

                    LUIS
(Luis goes in for a
handshake that ends in a
hug.)

Not good.

                    CESAR
What's up, Papa?

                    LUIS
I got hit today.

                    CESAR
In a fight?

GAYLE

Where is my Rhona? I have this great recipe…

CESAR

Shhh.

(Cesar shrugs)

We're talking.

GAYLE

I was asking him where my daughter is. Are you
OK, Luis?

LUIS

Yeah, I just…

CESAR

Follow me.

(Cesar motions for Luis to
follow him outside.)

CESAR

Sorry about that. So, what happened?

LUIS

Some guy came to the store with a gun. (Beat)
Look, I gotta go.

CESAR

Shit. Do you know who it was?

                    LUIS
I'm gonna find out.

                         (Luis looks down the
                         street.)

                    CESAR
Hey.

                    LUIS
Yeah.

                    CESAR
Let me know, alright? And wait a bit before you
tell Rhona.

                    LUIS
Yeah, I know. I gotta go figure this shit out. If
you get a call from downtown…

                    CESAR
I got you. Don't worry.

                         (Luis walks off into the
                         night. Cesar watches him a
                         while before entering the
                         bar again.)

ACT II, SCENE 4

Setting: A secluded parking lot where Finn's car and the others parked several yards away are illuminated by one streetlight.

VADIM

Mr. Finn, it's late. What do you want from me?

FINN

What, I can't just call my favorite customer?
How's business?

VADIM

You don't lock the doors and kick out your
favorite customer. I don't care who you are with
your loans…

FINN

Well, then, let me know when you want my locks
taken off.

> (Finn begins walking
> toward the back door of the
> car.)

VADIM

Hey, wait. You told me you had another buyer.

FINN
(Finn turns back.)

I do, but it works better when I sell that God-awful place to you two.

> VADIM
> (Smiles, laughs for a moment)

Listen, you ask how's business?

> (Vadim points at Finn, whistles into the darkness.)
> VADIM

It is really good.

> (Jerry walks up wearing blue jeans, a hat, and boots.)
>
> (Rigel the limo driver exits the car and watches the man closely.)

> FINN

I'm guessing he's with you…

> VADIM

My newest addition. You two haven't met?

> FINN

Can't say we have.

> VADIM

Your driver looks interested.

FINN

You interested?

RIGEL

Nice shirt.

JERRY

I'm sorry, what did you say?

> (Jerry takes a step toward
> the driver)

FINN

Vadim, hold back your muscle, please?

> (Vadim pats Jerry's chest.)

VADIM

Jerry, it's OK.

VADIM

See we can all get along. Jerry, tell him so he
knows my check's good.

JERRY

His check's good.

VADIM

Not about the check! About the deal.

JERRY

Who is he? I don't talk to people I don't know.

FINN

If you know him, you know me.

(Jerry looks at Vadim.)

VADIM

He's fine. Tell him.

JERRY

There's some big shit going on. So big that they hired me.
We'll have two more hits in the bag by the end of this
week. And that's not his word, it's mine. You'll get your
money.

FINN

Sounds good to me.

VADIM

Like the Federal Reserve, trust me.

FINN

I trust you. You know I'm just looking to get paid.

VADIM

You heard Jerry. After we dump these deals, I'll pay that
house off in cash.

FINN

That's what I like to hear.

ACT II, SCENE 5

Setting: A cafe on the corner of Main Street. The temperate winter has allowed various eating establishments to continue seating customers outside. Luis is walking, consumed in his thoughts. He rounds the corner into the alley behind his shop where he sees a man trying to enter the back door. Luis stops and then turns back, enters the café, and takes a seat. A waitress walks up to his table.

                    TINA
Hey there, Hun, how are you today?

                    LUIS
I'm doing well.
                    (Luis looks at her name
                    tag)

Tina, I'll take a cranberry juice.

                    TINA
Of course. Are you hungry, too?

                    LUIS
The juice is fine for now.

                    TINA
I'll leave the menu just in case.

                    (Tina smiles flirtatiously as
                    she walks away. Luis looks
                    down the alley at the man,
                    fixed on his every move.)

                    TINA
Here you go.

                    LUIS
Thanks a lot.

                    TINA
                    (Tina strokes her earring
                    and watches as Luis sips
                    his drink.)

So, do you live nearby.

                    LUIS
Yeah, I do business in town.

                    TINA
Ah. What kind of business?

                    LUIS
Collectables.

                    TINA
Nice, I don't mean to be a creep, you're just my
only table.

                    LUIS
Don't worry about it. You out anytime soon?

                    (Tina smiles.)

TINA

Ten minutes. I've been here all night.

LUIS

That's great. Could you give me a hand by any
chance?

TINA

Sure! What do you need?

LUIS

It'll be easy. You see that guy over there?

(Tina looks.)

TINA

Yeah, do you know 'em?

LUIS

For years.

(Luis smiles guiltily.)

He's my best friend and we're planning a surprise
party for him.

TINA

Awww. That's awesome. Do you need me to help
set up?

LUIS

No, we're all set up. He's just getting a little nosy
and I need you to keep him occupied.

TINA

You really think I can?

LUIS

A beautiful girl like you? You'll be a natural.

> (Tina removes her apron
> and adjusts her shirt. She is
> all smiles. Luis finishes his
> juice, stands, and puts his
> hand on Tina's shoulder.)

LUIS

Alright, so you walk on down and I'll stay here.
Try to keep his attention long enough that I can
sneak over and enter through that door.

TINA

That one there?

LUIS

That one there. Now, if he starts acting weird,
which he might, just strut your stuff a bit and
we'll be in like flint.

TINA

Ooh. I can't wait.

LUIS

Me neither.

TINA
(Tina walks down the alley
and up to the man.)

Hi there.

NAZAR

Hello.

TINA

As you can see, I'm going for a jog, but I can't
seem to remember where the park is.

(Nazar looks her up and
down.)

TINA

Maybe you can help me. Do you think it's that
way or over there?

NAZAR
(Nazar steps back from the
door nervously.)

Yeah, probably either way. Try over there.

TINA

You think? Oh alright. Hey, what's your name?

NAZAR

Uhm, Nazar. Look, I have somewhere to go right
now.

(Without being seen by
Nazar, Luis sneaks behind
the garbage dumpster that
sits against the brick wall.
Tina sees him but stays
calm.)

TINA

Don't let me keep you.

(Nazar begins turning.)

TINA

My name is Tina.

NAZAR
(Nazar sighs.)

OK. Nice to meet you.

TINA
You, too. You're very handsome by the way.

NAZAR

Not me.

(Just as Tina is sure Luis
will open the door or just
yell surprise, Luis grips a
mop with no head laying
against the brick wall and
raises it. Before anyone can
notice what is happening,
Luis crouches behind

Nazar and swings it swiftly
at the man's ribs.)

NAZAR

Ahhh, shit! You scumbag!

(Nazar's knees buckle and
he drops to the ground.
Tina grabs her chest and
screams. Luis grabs Nazar
and begins dragging him.
Tina runs away.)

NAZAR

You dumb shit!

LUIS
(Luis pulls a pistol from
Nazar's pocket and throws
it far away. He then swings
opens the back door.)

Happy birthday, you fuck!

(Luis throws him into the
doorway and slams the
door behind him.)

Setting: Interior of Luis's shop. It is dimly lit
except for the showcase in the center of the room.

NAZAR

You…you are gonna pay for this. Pay for this!

> (Luis delivers his fist to the
> man's face until it bleeds.
> His blind rage ends in him
> dragging Nazar kicking
> and screaming to his
> largest showcase.)

NAZAR

What are you doing?

(Silence)

NAZAR

What are you doing, you son of a bitch?

LUIS

Oh, you don't know?

> (Luis slides the door of the
> case open.)

LUIS

Lord, please forgive me.

NAZAR

> (Nazar tries crawling
> away.)

Help!

LUIS

Hey, I got ya.

(Nazar tries dialing his cell phone.)

LUIS

Get back here.

(Luis kicks the phone out of his hand and drags him back to the showcase.)

NAZAR

You bastard.

LUIS

Who me? You asked for this, my friend.

NAZAR

Don't do this. You don't have to.

LUIS

You didn't have to take my fucking deal! I bought it. I did all the hard work!

(Luis kicks him in the ribs.)

NAZAR

You idiot! That was my brother.

LUIS

Brother huh? I was an only child, but I respect the whole sibling thing.

NAZAR

What?

(Luis slaps him. He then
slumps Nazar's wiggling
body over his knee and
forces him into the
showcase.)

NAZAR

Please let me out! I don't know anything.

LUIS

I know. That's why you're here.

NAZAR

You're gonna be sorry when we kill you.

(Luis slides the door shut.
He stands with tears
running from his eyes and
walks paranoid around his
shop before finally slipping
out the door.)

("ALMOST UNCIRCULATED")

ACT III, SCENE 1

Setting: Rhona's office at the newspaper headquarters. The place is a bit scattered, but in working order. Rhona's mom Gayle sits on a couch across from Rhona with a satchel style purse. Gayle gulps down water from a cup. Rhona stands looking at her laptop.

GAYLE

Thank you, Love, I needed that.

RHONA

Mhm.

GAYLE

I'm in love with that dress. Wow.

RHONA

Oh, this? Ann made it.

GAYLE

Ann? With the stupid horse?

RHONA

Hey, I liked that horse. It added a bit of prestige to main street.

GAYLE

Whatever you say. She's a good seamstress, I'll give her that.

RHONA
(Rhona shakes her head.)

So, what brought you to this side of town?

GAYLE
Honey, I just wanted to see the place. You're
moving up so fast.

RHONA
I love it. (Beat) It just never stops though, Mom.

GAYLE
You wanted to be a journalist.

RHONA
Yeah, with a typewriter and a cigarette. This is
just...

GAYLE
It's different today, Hun. All the news just flies
by.

RHONA
Yeah. Sometimes this local paper feels more like
a tabloid. And Luis can't stand hearing about the
drama.

GAYLE
He better be devoted to you, I know how he gets
with that business.

RHONA

Mom, he is very fervent when it comes to the
store. (Beat) Shoot! I just remembered, I have to
call him back.

(Gayle rolls her eyes.
Rhona dials the phone.)

Setting: Voice-over conversation.

RHONA

I'm so sorry about that. I still have so much to do
on the waterfront story.

LUIS

That's fine. Are you free tonight? I'm gotta go
back and meet with Mrs. Bensin.

RHONA

Uhm, yeah. Didn't you meet with her?

LUIS

Yeah! Apparently, she forgot one... I don't
know.

RHONA

Sure, Sweetie. I can head home and pack some
food for the ride.

LUIS

Don't worry, I got it.

RHONA

K, mister. I'll meet you at the gas station.

ACT III, SCENE 2

Setting: Luis is parked out front of a convenience store. The place is quiet and the road out front is free of any traffic. Luis looks around waiting for Rhona to arrive.

RHONA

Honey!

> (Rhona walks into frame
> alongside of the building.)

Luis, over here.

LUIS
> (Luis looks back then
> finally spots her.)

Oh, hey.

RHONA

Are you OK?

LUIS

Yeah. Why? What's up?

RHONA

I don't know, you sounded off on the phone.

LUIS

Nah. (Beat) You need anything from inside?

RHONA

Oh, yeah. I forgot. Hold that.

(Rhona hands the tote bag
to Luis.)

LUIS

Here.

RHONA

You sure, Honey? I have the card.

LUIS
(Distantly)

Whatever.

(Rhona grabs the cash and
walks toward the store.
Once she is out of sight,
Luis grabs his phone and
sees five missed calls from
Finn.)

LUIS

Really, Finn? Five fucking calls?

(Luis looks around then
puts the phone to his ear.)

LUIS

Hello?

FINN
(Voice-over.)

Are you fucking nuts or is it just the Puerto Rican in you?

LUIS

What do you mean?

FINN

I just received a call from the police that a dead Ukrainian man was found stuffed in a showcase at your store.

(Luis rubs his head.)

FINN

Ring any bells, brother?

LUIS

Yes, yes… Look, I'm sorry I killed him, but you told me…

FINN

Hey, I understand. I'm sure he deserved it. But I clearly asked you something last night and I'm pretty sure you remember what it was.

LUIS

I know, I thought I had it.

FINN

Well now you look all fucked up. I'm telling you.

LUIS

I get it.

FINN

Now you look less like a shop owner being
robbed and more like a fucking psychopath.

LUIS

Finn, I'm sorry, OK? Shit!

FINN

It doesn't matter. These guys are meeting with
their new addition tonight.

LUIS

What does that mean?

FINN

It's not fucking good.

> (Car area of set goes dim
> and Rhona is lit up stage
> right.)

LUIS

Hey, let me call you back.

RHONA

Ma, listen. I just took the test and
it...yes...yes... Why don't you let me talk? It
says here that I'm pregnant.

(Rhona paces and listens.)

RHONA

Yeah, Mom, I'll call you back.

(Luis now speaks from
inside the car to Iggy who
is posing as a worker.)

IGGY

I'm so sorry, buddy. We have to ask you to pull
around back.

LUIS

What are you talking about?

IGGY

We have a truck coming in now and you can't be
hanging out here.

LUIS

Who said I was hanging out?

RHONA

Luis, the man inside said we have to pull around
because of a delivery.

LUIS

Yeah, but we're about to leave. Why does that
matter to me?

IGGY

I'm sorry guy. There's an exit around back.

RHONA
(Rhona enters the car.)

Come on! Let's just go.

LUIS

Fucking seriously? Fine.

> (Luis pulls his car around
> back to a more secluded
> area. Luis exits the car. He
> throws his arms up.)

Around back! You happy?

RHONA

Honey, get in here.

LUIS
(Luis looks around and
spots a car in the distance.
A man pulls a gun from his
jacket and shoots at Luis.
Luis ducks down next to
the car.)

What the fuck!

                              RHONA
Luis! What's happening?

                              LUIS
I don't know. Are you OK?

                              (The man shoots again.
                              Luis creeps over and opens
                              Rhona's door.)

                              LUIS
Come here.

                              RHONA
I'm scared.

                              LUIS
Just come here.

                              RHONA
I can't find my phone.

                              LUIS
Forget the phone, Rhona.

                              (Rhona shakes as she slips
                              out of the door and
                              crouches next to Luis.)

                              LUIS
Hey, asshole. Who are you?

(Silence.)

LUIS

Hello! Who the fuck are you?

(Rhona shakes as she holds
her husband's arm tightly.)

IGGY

No need to know. You took my father. You know
who we are.

RHONA

Baby, baby! What is he talking about?

LUIS

So, fucking me over is a family business, huh?

IGGY

Yes. Now come out!

LUIS

What, so you can act like you know how to fire
that gun again?

(Iggy, arguing with Jerry,
fires again and hits the
chrome bumper.)

LUIS

You really have a God damn death wish, don't
you?

JERRY

You kill ours; we kill yours!

> (Jerry pushes Iggy aside
> and starts walking around
> the car. Iggy pulls his
> shirt.)

JERRY

Get, off me!

LUIS

> (Luis pops the trunk.)

You better stop walking.

JERRY

Stop walking? Says who?

RHONA

Call the police.

LUIS

Shhh!

> (Jerry looks cautiously.
> Luis nervously shuffles
> through the trunk.)

LUIS

I said stop fucking walking!

(Luis pulls out his fishing
rod with a big, weighted
snag hook from the trunk.)

JERRY

Alright, get out here pretty boy.

(Jerry points the pistol
around the car.)

LUIS

Eat it, cowboy!

(Luis whacks Jerry in the
face with the end of the
fishing rod. Jerry grabs his
face.)

JERRY

Ahhh, asshole!

(Luis casts the big gaff
hook toward Iggy. Jerry
flinches and then watches
the hook drop behind
Iggy.)

JERRY

Shit, Iggy, watch out!

IGGY

What the hell is…

(The hook hops up, buries
itself in Iggy's throat, and

Luis begins reeling the
monofilament line like a
tournament winner.

IGGY

Oh no, Jerry, oh no...

(Iggy stumbles and then
awkwardly speed walks
toward Jerry. Jerry steps
quickly up to him and
grabs his shoulder.)

JERRY

Iggy, you OK? Hey, hey, hey! Shit!

(Luis stands with wide
eyes. Rhona shakes as she
steps away from him
slowly. Iggy drops to the
ground)

JERRY

You son of a... He's gonna die!!!

(Luis nods his head
slowly.)

JERRY

Look what you did!

(Rhona walks back toward
Luis. Luis holds the
passenger door open and

Rhona enters glaring at the
enemy.)

JERRY

He's dying, you fucking spick!

LUIS
(Angry, but calm, Luis
walks around to the driver's
side.)

Well, then you better fucking bury him. Because
as you know, there's a truck coming and…

(Luis pauses to look
around)

…the only exit is around back.

(Luis puts his arms up and
looks side to side.)

JERRY

You're gonna wish you didn't do this, Mr. Luis.

LUIS

All I'm gonna wish is that I cast that hook twice.

(Luis enters the car and
then pulls away.)

ACT III, SCENE 3

Setting: Music from an ice cream truck plays in the background. The Bensin house on the outskirts of town is lit up by the afternoon sun. Luis and Rhona stand on a large porch talking and waiting.

RHONA

I can't believe you.

> (Luis looks broken. He has
> no words.)

RHONA

I can't believe you put me through that. Where do I start with you, Luis? Where do I fucking start?

LUIS

I'm sorry, Rhona.

RHONA

You can say sorry when you explain.

LUIS

I...look so...Alright.

RHONA

Oh, my God! Say something. Make up the lie, go ahead.

LUIS

I'm not lying about anything! Those guys are out
to kill me.

RHONA

That part's pretty clear, Sweetie.

LUIS

OK, you remember the day I went to sell that
collection?

RHONA

Yesterday?

LUIS

Uh, yeah. I got there and the fucking guy...

RHONA

What guy?

LUIS

I don't know. But he had a gun. And, and, and...

(Luis starts panicking.)

RHONA

Hey, calm down.

LUIS

And if it wasn't for Finn, I'd be dead right now.

RHONA

Finn? Is this Finn's fault? He is done. I'm calling
the police.

LUIS

Stop!

        (Luis puts his hand up)

I killed the guy. It's my fault.

RHONA

Wait. You killed someone? Why was this a
secret, Luis?

LUIS

I am sorry! You've never kept a secret from me?

RHONA

Yep. I'm pregnant.

        (Luis's eyes grow wide.
        Mrs. Bensin walks up
        quietly behind the couple.
        She is carrying a bag from
        the store.)

MRS. BENSIN

If you two keep arguing, I'll make you wash the
dishes.

        (Luis and Rhona are
        startled, but quickly begin

sweet-talking Mrs. Bensin.)

                    RHONA
Don't worry about us. We can never decide
where to eat when we're out this way.

                 MRS. BENSIN
I'll do it for you, you're eating here.

                    RHONA
Are you sure? You're so sweet. Are there any
more groceries?

                 MRS. BENSIN
Nope, this is it.

               (All four enter the house.)

(The interior of the house is decorated with slightly aged,
yet beautiful furniture.)

                    RHONA
Wow, what a beautiful place Mrs. B.

                 MRS. BENSIN
Ha! It looks old to me.

                    RHONA
No, I think…

                 MRS. BENSIN
But thank you, honey. Have a seat.

LUIS

Oh, sure.

MRS. BENSIN

I didn't know you'd come so soon. I left the
message, but I thought with being busy and
everything.

RHONA

That's just it. Between being married to him and
running the paper, I need a day off.

MRS. BENSIN

You're too sweet. I'm happy you chose to come
here (laughs). And you're welcome to take a load
off however you want.

> (Luis and Rhona trade
> glances.)

LUIS

Could I check out the yard? I mean, if you don't
need help putting things away.

MRS. BENSIN

Go ahead but watch out for the groundskeeper. I
think he's sleeping on the porch.

LUIS

You sure? It's fine if...

RHONA

Hun, go ahead.

MRS. BENSIN

Don't worry. If you wake him, he'll just bend your ear for an hour before you can even get a word in.

> (Luis shrugs and then
> walks out the back door.)

GROUNDSKEEPER

Sue, this groundhog keeps startin' with me. One minute he's out there, then I see him tear-assing to the shed. I don't care if he makes a home, but what about the books in there.

LUIS

Uhm. Hey, sir, how are you?

GROUNDSKEEPER

Pretty good, son. I thought you were Mrs. Bensin.

LUIS

You must be her groundskeeper?

GROUNDSKEEPER

Yeah, that's me I suppose. How are you today?

> (Luis and the
> groundskeeper shake
> hands.)

LUIS

I'm alright. (Beat) I'm here with my wife to visit
Mrs. Bensin. Man, it's nice out here.

GROUNDSKEEPER

Thank you. Have a seat. Stay a few.

> (Luis sits in a seat a few
> feet from the
> groundskeeper.)

So, you and your lady work together?

LUIS

No, she works for the Beacon.

GROUNDSKEEPER

That's the, uh, local one?

LUIS

Yeah.

GROUNDSKEEPER

That's great. Have you ever done any business
with Mrs. Bensin?

LUIS

Yeah. I bought some of her husband's stuff a few
days ago.

GROUNDSKEEPER

I heard. He had some good stuff, huh?

LUIS
(Luis takes a deep breath
thinking back on the last 24
hours.)

He sure did, sir. Maybe too good.

GROUNDSKEEPER
Well, I hope the collection treats you well.

LUIS
Thank you.

GROUNDSKEEPER
(The groundskeeper
struggles a moment and
then stands. He steps out to
the edge of the porch and
looks out over the land and
setting sun. Luis watches
him.)

You see that business of yours is quite
interesting.

LUIS
Sure can be.

All that gold and silver being bought and sold. It
makes you feel pretty damn strong.

(Luis shakes his head in
agreement.)

GROUNDSKEEPER

I always thought it was funny how the faces on my pocket change would never have a damn clue how important they would be today. (Pause) It makes you wonder. Such an elite type of thing that you'll just never be a part of until you quit being scared and buy your first coin.

LUIS

I never thought that way.

GROUNDSKEEPER

But then again, it's not all that hard. It's an education like anything else.

(Luis is confused.)

GROUNDSKEEPER

Your name again, son?

LUIS

Luis, sir.

GROUNDSKEEPER
(The groundskeeper holds his hand out for a shake. Luis stands and shakes.)

Mr. Bensin. Nice to meet you.

LUIS
(Luis looks into the man's eyes with bewilderment. The handshake breaks off.)

I thought…Mrs. Bensin said that…

HERMAN BENSIN
No. Don't tell me. I can just imagine what she said. (Beat) She never took to the collection.

LUIS
(Luis shakes his head.)

Look, if she didn't mean to sell them I can…I can try to return them.

HERMAN BENSIN
Hey, if she did any damn thing I'm sure she meant it. And besides, that means you're the one who read the letter.

LUIS
(Breathes deeply, bites his lip)
Yeah.

HERMAN BENSIN
Oh, man, where did you learn?

LUIS
What? The business?

HERMAN BENSIN
Mhm.

LUIS

My uncle. He was the first Hispanic coin dealer on our side of town.

HERMAN BENSIN

Who, Montanez? I knew 'em.

LUIS

You did?

HERMAN BENSIN

That was my side of town, too.

LUIS

Damn.

HERMAN BENSIN

He passed on, didn't he?

LUIS

Yeah…

HERMAN BENSIN

You have any kids yet yourself?

LUIS

None yet. But we just found out there's one on the way.

(Luis smiles.)

HERMAN BENSIN

Oh man. You must be floating on that news.

LUIS

It's a lot, but I'm excited.

HERMAN BENSIN
(Herman walks to the
railing.)

So, can I trust that you'll make a promise with me
on such a clear night? I mean the sun only paints
a picture like this once in a while.

LUIS

Anything you wish, sir.

HERMAN BENSIN
(Herman turns toward
Luis. He flips a coin and
catches it in his open hand
extended toward Luis.)

I'm gonna give you this coin you came here for…

(He places it in Luis's
hand.)

HERMAN BENSIN

And you're gonna give it to that bundle of joy
someday or since things do change, you will use
it to make that kid as happy as you can.

(Luis is wide-eyed and
listening.)

HERMAN BENSIN

I mean, you don't have to spoil 'em none.

LUIS

You're right.

HERMAN BENSIN

Just take it and teach them a thing or two. Ballet lessons or a baseball glove.

> (Luis studies the coin.)

> (Auctioneer voice-over: "Do I hear 3-2-5? Anyone, 3-2-5? Sold for three hundred thousand dollars to bidder 4-7-9.")

> LUIS
> (Luis cranes his neck up and to the side until his eyes meet Herman's. Herman winks at him.)

But Mr. Bensin, (beat) do you know what this goes for? It's almost uncirculated.

HERMAN BENSIN

I've had this coin since 1966. I'm pretty sure I know what it goes for son.

> (Herman grins at Luis and then sits. He takes a sip from his coffee.)

LUIS

Are you serious?

HERMAN BENSIN

Don't I look it?

LUIS

Yeah, I mean it'll be my honor. Thank you so much.

HERMAN BENSIN

Hey, I won't be put in a mummy box with my rubies and my diamonds. A guy like you deserves to make use of it.

LUIS

I sure will. But what do I tell the ladies inside.

HERMAN BENSIN

Easy, tell Mrs. Bensin it was worth fifty bucks. All that flipping, I wore the face right off. As for your wife, tell her what you want when you leave. It's yours now.

LUIS

How can I repay you?

HERMAN BENSIN

We made a promise. Keep it.

LUIS

OK.

HERMAN BENSIN

And get yourself full on the food in there. If you don't eat, she'll probably wait till you leave and blame me for it.

LUIS

Gotcha. Thanks again, Herman.

> (Luis enters through the back door.)

ACT III, SCENE 4

Setting: The interior hallway of the house. Luis walks through the back door shaking his head. Rhona appears.

RHONA

Hey.

LUIS
(Startled)

Oh, shit! Hey!

RHONA

How's everything going?

LUIS

Uhm, good. What about you?

RHONA

Did you do the deal?

LUIS

I guess…

RHONA

What do you mean? Did you have to pay a lot?

LUIS

Nothing.

RHONA

Wait, so we came all the way here…

(Luis holds out his hand
with the coin.)

RHONA

How did…?

LUIS

This (beat) was Mr. Bensin's coin.

RHONA

Yeah, and what about it?

LUIS

And he gave it to me.

RHONA

I thought he was dead.

LUIS

No. Mrs. Bensin lied.

RHONA

What? I can't believe that.

LUIS

Right? I saw one of these sell last month for three
hundred thousand.

RHONA

Holy shit. But if he knew why didn't he make
you pay?

LUIS

He asked if we had any kids. He said it was a gift
to help raise our baby. I asked if he was sure and
he just said that she never took him seriously.

RHONA

Are you sure he doesn't have a problem?

LUIS

He is all there, Rhona. I love you so much and I
am so sorry, but we have to get out of here.

RHONA

You're right, Baby.

(The couple embrace then
a loud crash of the screen
door is heard. They both
turn to look.)

RHONA

What was that?

MRS. BENSIN

Hey guys? I think someone's here.

(A gunshot sounds.)

LUIS

Damn it! Wait here.

(Luis opens the door and
runs out.)

(A small spotlight
illuminates Vadim on stage
left. He walks toward
Rhona.)

VADIM

There you are, honey.

RHONA

Who the hell are you?

VADIM

I heard you were quite the pretty one when you
and your man killed my Iggy.

RHONA
(Rhona turns.)

Luis!

VADIM
(Vadim grabs her sweater.)
Hey!

RHONA
You're right and he fucking deserved it.

VADIM
Alright, alright. I apologize. But I did overhear
that you're pregnant. Is this true?

(Vadim backs the young
lady up to the wall.)

You'll be a beautiful mama if you ask me.

LUIS
(Luis swings the screen
door open. He then looks at
the two.)
You asshole!

(Vadim laughs.)

LUIS
(Luis lunges between the
two. Vadim grabs him and
swings him around his
hip.)

Ahh, get the fu…

(Luis hits the ground hard.)

VADIM

Ah, back to revenge.

            (Vadim makes a tight fist
            and launches it into
            Rhona's stomach.)

            RHONA

No! Why??? You piece of shit.

            LUIS
            (Luis struggles to pull his
            head up but after seeing his
            wife writhing in pain he
            launches up from the
            floor.)

You want to die tonight, don't you? You
motherfucker!

            (Luis runs at Vadim with
            both hands out. He jumps
            on Vadim like an animal.)

            LUIS

Ahhh! I'm gonna break you!

            (Both men drop to the
            ground. Luis chokes him as
            Vadim fights back.)

            VADIM

You…are a joke.

LUIS

So start laughing!

(Luis scoots up and
straddles the Vadim's
chest. He begins punching
the man maniacally. Left,
right, left right, twenty
times before tiring out.)

VADIM

Ahhh!

LUIS
(Luis's last punch crashes
onto the hardwood floor
and he shakes off the pain.
Vadim sees his opportunity
and lunges up landing a
head-butt on Luis's
forehead.)

Ah! Coño!

(Luis dizzily circles his
head trying to see straight.
Vadim watches him.)

FINN
(Finn then enters through
the kitchen doorway, pulls
his jacket back and draws a
small German pistol. He

then grabs Luis under his
ribs and flips him off
Vadim.)

Go on. Join your brother.

(He blows Vadim's
memories out the back of
his head.)

(Sirens grow loud as the set
dims.)

(The exterior of Mrs.
Bensin's house is quiet
with one tall light
illuminating the set. Two
officers walk up to Finn as
he smokes his cigarette.
Finn brushes his medium
hair back.)

OFFICER DOYLE
Good evening, Mr. Finn. What are we up to?

FINN
Officer Doyle, everything you need to know is
right here.

(Officer Doyle grabs the
fully written police report
from Finn as the second
officer arrives.)

OFFICER ZAREMBA
What is that? Does Sheriff Brown know what's
happening?

OFFICER DOYLE
Sheriff Brown, Finn and myself go way back. If
it's here, it's the truth.

(Officer Zaremba looks
confused.)

OFFICER DOYLE
But we do need to section this place off. Both
homeowners are dead?

FINN
Yeah. Not so pretty. Follow me.

(The two officers follow
Finn through the side door
and into the hallway.
Officer Doyle tries
consoling Rhona while
Luis sits on the hallway
chair with his head down.)

OFFICER ZAREMBA
Shit, what happened? (Beat) Sorry ma'am, it just
looks like they both lost.

FINN
(Finn reaches into his
pocket.)

You want to know what happened? That fucking clown there tried to rob my friend of this coin.

OFFICER DOYLE

Self-defense, huh?

OFFICER ZAREMBA

But all that over one little coin?

FINN

This coin is worth more than your house, buddy.

OFFICER ZAREMA

Hah, I don't know about that.

FINN

Three hundred thousand buys it if you're interested.

> (Zaremba shuts his mouth
> and looks around at the
> framed photographs. Doyle
> steps up to Luis.)

OFFICER DOYLE

I am so sorry. People are evil these days.

LUIS

They sure are. I just wish you could have stopped these guys before all this.

OFFICER DOYLE

I do too.

LUIS
(Luis walks up to his wife
and puts his arm around
her. He looks into her
eyes.)

We'll go to the doctor tomorrow. See if anything
can be done.

RHONA
Thank you.

(The couple embraces for a
short time.)

FINN
Hey, sorry. Can we talk?

(Luis nods.)

FINN
We're gonna step outside, boys.

(Officer Doyle waves in
acceptance. Finn leads the
couple back to the front of
the house.)

FINN
So, look guys, I'm sorry all of this happened.

(Finn pauses.)

But, Rhona, if I didn't get him out of that store,
we'd be meeting at his funeral.

RHONA

I understand. I just don't get why you didn't call
the police when this started.

(Rhona wipes her eyes.)

FINN

They aren't worth a damn.

(Rhona looks at Luis.)

LUIS

He's right.

FINN

Those cops in there. They won't do shit one way
or another. You know, you work for the
newspaper.

RHONA

I guess. I don't know anymore.

FINN

Now while we're here and you can be his ears,
we have to talk.

LUIS

Go ahead.

                        FINN
Here's your coin.

                              (Luis takes the coin and
                              places it deep in his
                              pocket.)

                        FINN
And here's your gun. (Beat) Don't lie to me
again.

                        LUIS
I'm sorry.

                        FINN
It's easier to pay off the cops than to pay for a
fucking headstone.

                              (Rhona grasps Luis's arm
                              tightly.)

                        FINN
It's legal. Don't worry about it.

                        LUIS
Thank you, brother.

                        FINN
Any time. This should all be over, but just be
careful. The scum tends to stick together.

                        FINN
                      (To Rhona)

And you. Be careful out there. Keep this guy in line.

> (Rhona nods yes. Finn walks out to the road and lights a cigarette. He then whistles for his car. Just then, Finn is dropped by a bullet coming from across the street. He grips his stomach tightly.)

                    LUIS

Shit!

                    RHONA
> (Rhona runs over and kneels next to Finn.)

Finn! Are you OK?

> (Jerry walks out from the shadows and toward the group. Luis draws his gun.)

                    FINN

Ahhh! Fucking come on!

> (Officer Doyle runs out from inside.)

             OFFICER DOYLE

Stop right there!

(Jerry shoots him. He drops
to the ground. He then
walks up to Rhona and
aims his gun at her.)

JERRY

Hey there, friend.

LUIS

Put the fucking gun down!

JERRY

You look prettier with all that makeup running.

LUIS

I will fucking shoot you!

JERRY

I can't spend time with the baby momma?

LUIS

That's it! You're dead!

(Luis steps quickly toward
Jerry.)

JERRY

No! I'm actually not!

(Jerry points his pistol
straight at Luis.)

You see, you helped me kill all these stupid fucking guys, but now I can run it the way it should be.

(Jerry clicks the revolver's hammer back.)

So, won't you help me run it?

CESAR
(Cesar walks with gun in hand from across the road. Luis looks up quickly but then notices who it is. Cesar points his gun at Jerry.)

Sorry, amigo.

(He shoots Jerry in the head. He drops to the ground and Rhona runs crying into Luis's arms.)

RHONA
Baby...Oh God, Baby...

LUIS
You're OK, Honey. It's OK.

CESAR
(Cesar squats next to Finn. He caresses his head.)

It's alright, Papa. You're gonna be OK.

FINN

Luis. Get me…out of here.

LUIS

I got you buddy. Just keep those eyes open.

ACT III, SCENE 5

Setting: Dark stage, spotlight on Luis. The audience at book reading is seated in front of him. Luis paces around the stage.

LUIS

I'm sorry guys.

> (Luis softly picks up one of his books and studies it before dropping it back on the table. He then grabs the corner of the table, picks it up, and slams it back down. Luis speaks, sobbing.)

LUIS

Five years and it doesn't get any easier… Thank you for coming.

> (Luis sits down on his chair with his head in his hands. A five-year-old boy walks

up and rubs his back. Luis
looks up and then back
down. He puts his arm
around the boy and draws
him closer.)

(The set dims around Luis
and his son. Finn enters
from stage left, smoking a
cigarette. He blows smoke
and then begins speaking.)

FINN

Man, I'm…

(Finn draws a deep breath.)

I'm never good at this kind of thing. I mean, what
can I say? You'd be broken, too, if you went
through the same stuff he did. But anyway, it
could have been a lot worse looking back. He
could've been shot down. His wife, too. That kid
could have been born braindead.

(Finn pauses)

But instead this happens.

(Finn looks over shoulder.)

And it makes sense. The guy did emotionally
destroy his family. He didn't ask for it. But she
did what she thought was right and walked away
from him.

The way I see it, we're all just buying and re-
selling moments. Memories. Pleading to buy
back the shiny ones we lost along the way. And
the only catch is that we're still just children like
him looking through keyholes slightly higher
than eye level. So, we stand on an old basketball
or some sharp rocks we piled up just to catch a
glimpse of those moments. Just to hear a solitary
note from a song that once played on a boombox
somewhere in the middle of summer.

You know,

     (Finn laughs.)

I shoulda wrote this thing…

They'll be alright though.

     (Rhona walks up and grabs
     the boy's arm. Luis and
     Rhona lock eyes.)

Her, too. Just give it some time and she'll be
holding an umbrella over his head at the kid's
graduation. As it pisses rain and everyone's eyes
are fixed on the stage, they'll share a kiss and
swear that it never happened.

     (Finn slowly walks off
     stage.)

     FADE TO BLACK.

     THE END.

www.ingramcontent.com/pod-product-compliance
Lightning Source LLC
Chambersburg PA
CBHW031838170626
46807CB00004B/1521